Baby Knows Best

by Kathy Henderson

Illustrated by Brita Granström

Little, Brown and Company
Boston New York London

We gave the baby rattles
and we gave her things with bells
she's got toys that roll and click and tick;
there's one that sings as well.
She's got a sorting box that whistles
and a squeaky mouse to squeeze . . .

For Annie, Daniel, Charley, Nick and Ruth,
and all the other babies who know best K.H.

For Björn with love   B.G.

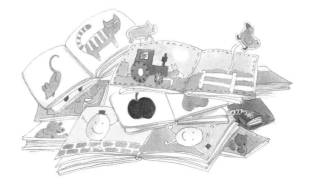

Text copyright © 2001 by Kathy Henderson
Illustrations copyright © 2001 by Brita Granström

First U.S. Edition

First published by
Transworld Publishers
61-63 Uxbridge Road
London W5 5SA
England

ISBN 0-316-60580-8
LCCN 00-107325

10 9 8 7 6 5 4 3 2 1

Printed in Singapore

And what does she want to play with?

The front door keys.

She's got a cloth book about farms
that's full of ducks and pigs and goats,
she's got my old book of nursery rhymes,
and a plastic book that floats.
She's got books with cardboard pages
and bright pictures just for her . . .

And what does she want to look at?

The newspaper.

Grandpa brought a bath toy
that's got sieves and scoops inside;
he brought a wind-up swimming hippo
with a mouth that opens wide.
She already had a tugboat
and a duck-shaped glug-glug jug . . .

But what does she want at bath time?

The old bath plug.

She's got dungarees and trousers,
she's got diapers, tights, and socks,
she's got a bright pink quilted snow suit
and two flower-patterned smocks.
She's got more clothes than we have
even though she's very small . . .

And what does she like wearing best?

Nothing at all.

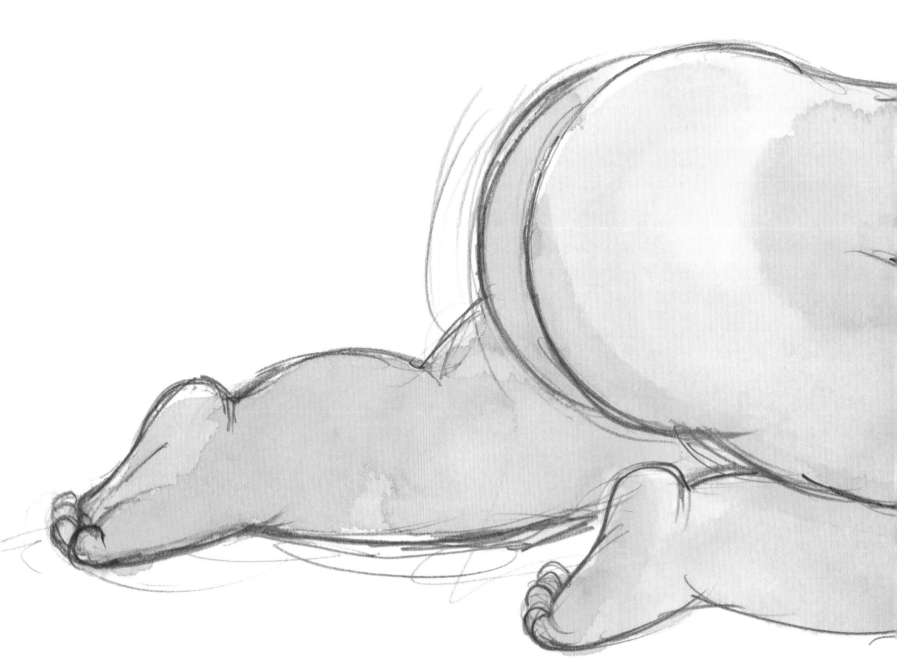

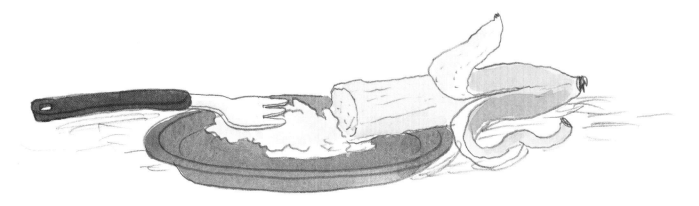

We mash up ripe bananas
and turn carrots into soup.
We buy jars of special baby mush
and powdered packet gloop.
We give her teething rusks and finger food
but she just drops the lot.

'Cause what d'you think she wants to eat?

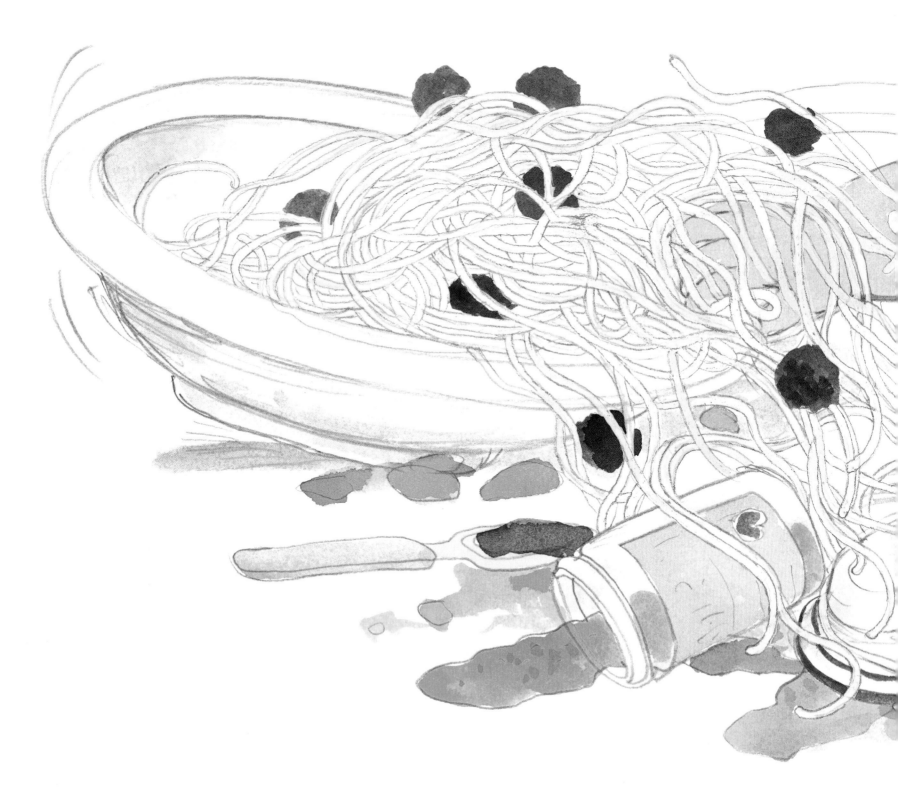

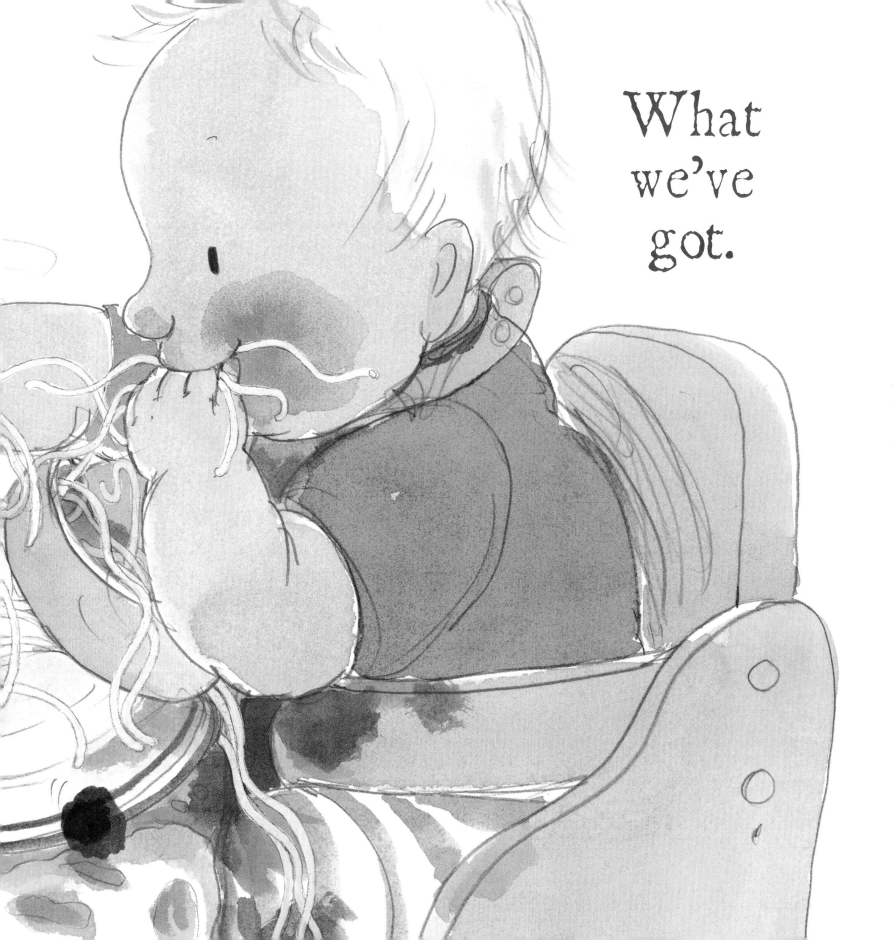

What
we've
got.

She has a stroller and a backpack
and a carriage up on wheels;
then there's her car seat with the handle
and the string of colored bells,
and her high chair and the bouncer
and the crib. There's all this stuff . . .

And where does she want to be?

Snuggled up with us.